Roger Takes Charge!

D1486996

First published in the United States by
Dial Books for Young Readers
A Division of Penguin Books USA Inc.
2 Park Avenue
New York, New York 10016
Published in Great Britain by the Bodley Head
Copyright © 1987 by Susanna Gretz
All rights reserved
Library of Congress Catalog Card Number: 86-24061
Printed in Hong Kong
First Pied Piper Printing 1990
N
1 2 3 4 5 6 7 8 9 10

A Pied Piper Book is a registered trademark of
Dial Books for Young Readers,
a division of Penguin Books USA Inc.,
® TM 1,163,686 and ® TM 1,054,312.

ROGER TAKES CHARGE!
is published in a hardcover edition by
Dial Books for Young Readers.
ISBN 0-8037-0742-8

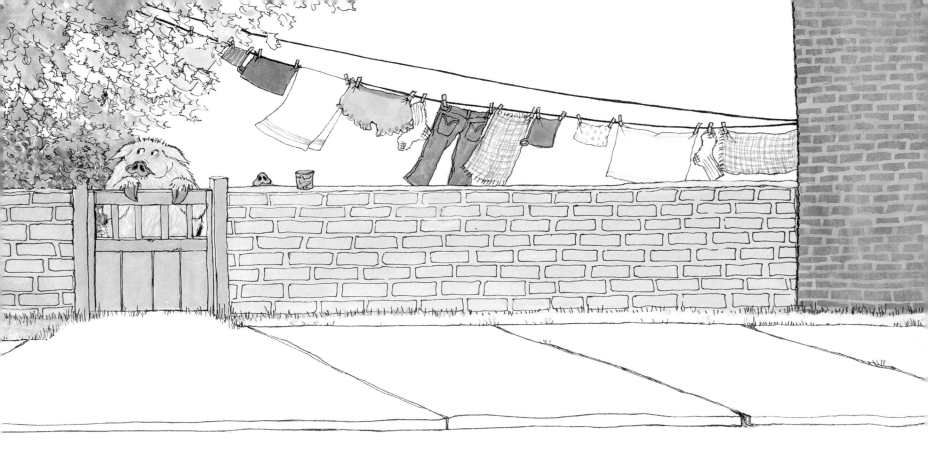

Roger Takes Charge!

Susanna Gretz

Dial Books for Young Readers / *New York*

Roger is staying at home with his little brother, Nelson.

"Do I *have* to look after him?" he grumbles.

"Yes," says his mother, "and while I'm out, Roger, you're in charge. Be good!"

"Don't worry," says her friend Mrs. Sauberman. "My daughter Flo is *always* good. She'll keep an eye on them both."

"Right. I'm in charge," says Flo.
"We're going to play I Spy.
I spy something blue
and you get three guesses."

Roger thinks hard.
"Is it the jeans?" he asks.
   "No."
   "Is it the garbage can?"
   "No."
   "Is it the sky?"
   "*No*, and that's your last guess!"

"What *else* is blue then?"
asks Roger.

Let's play
Hide-and-Seek!

"The mattress, of course, dumbo!" says Flo. "My turn again.
I spy with my little eye something pink, and this time,
I'll give you *five* guesses."

Just one little game!
Please, Roger!

"Is it the roses?" asks Roger.
"No."
"Is it Nelson's cup?"
"No."
"Is it the gate?"
"No."
"Is it the paper in the garbage can?"
"No."
"Is it the pants on the clothesline?"
"No, and that's your last guess."
"What *else* is pink, then?" asks Roger.

"*You* are, of course, stupid!" says Flo. "I've won again!
Come on, now I'll race you to the tree!

PLEASE!

Ready, get set . . . go!"

"I've won!" says Flo.
"Beat you to the top of the tree.

Ready, get set . . . go!"

When you come down can we play Hide-and-Seek, Roger?

"I've won *again*," says Flo.
"Now watch me land on the mattress.

That's scary.

Ready, get set . . . go!''

"Beat that, Roger!" says Flo.
"Now it's your turn.

"Right!" says Roger.
"Now *I'm* in charge and we're going
to play Hide-and-Seek."
    "You'll never find me," says Flo.
    "You just wait!" says Roger.

Roger hides his eyes, while Flo and Nelson look for hiding places. "1 . . . 2 . . . 3 . . . 4 . . ." counts Roger.

"...98...99...100! Ready or not, here I come!"

"I can see you, Nelson," Roger yells.

"*Honestly*, Flo!" says Mrs. Sauberman.
"Just look at you! You're filthy!
What *have* you been up to —"
"She's been looking after us," says Nelson.

"Bye, Flo," says Roger. "See you tomorrow!"

Susanna Gretz

was born in New York and grew up in New Jersey. After working for the Red Cross and living for a while in Germany, she moved to England and now lives in West London. She has written and illustrated three books for Dial: *It's Your Turn, Roger!*; *Roger Takes Charge!*, an IRA-CBC Children's Choice; and *Roger Loses His Marbles!*